The Boy a

Catherine Storr is a very ...
children's books as well as se...
with three grown-up daught...
London and currently...

Jonathan
Rogers

The Boy
and the Swan

illustrated by Laszlo Acs

Catherine Storr

Piper Books

First publish 1987 by André Deutsch Limited
This Piper edition published 1988 by Pan Books Ltd,
Cavaye Place, London sw10 9pg
9 8 7 6 5 4 3
© Catherine Storr 1987
Illustrations © André Deutsch Limited 1987
All rights reserved
isbn 0 330 30426 7
Printed and bound in Great Britain by
Richard Clay Ltd, Bungay, Suffolk

for Hugo

I

At school, the other children sometimes asked the boy
questions which he could not answer.

'Why don't you live with your Mum? Or your Dad?'

'Because I don't,' he said.

'Who do you live with then?'

'My Gran.' But he was not sure if she was really his Gran.

'Haven't you got a Mum or a Dad?'

'I don't live with them,' the boy said.

'What's your Gran like?'

'She's old,' the boy said. He did not say that she was also
deaf. When he had first come to the village school, the other
children had found it difficult to understand what he said.
The old woman whom he called his Gran spoke in a loud, flat
voice, and he had done the same, shouting to try to make her
hear. Because he was quick at learning, he had soon copied
the other children and for years now he had talked as they
did. But he did not like their questions and he spoke to them
as little as he could. He did not live in the little town where he
went to school, but walked two miles every morning and two
miles back to the cottage which had been his and the old
woman's home ever since he could remember.

The cottage was one of a huddle of small buildings between

the sea shore and the flat, marshy country behind the dunes. A short way down the road there was a duckpond, a telephone box and a small shop which sold newspapers and cigarettes and sweets and was also a sub-post-office. The long shore was sandy, with wooden breakwaters running down across it, to curb the sullen fury of the grey North Sea. But the sea was not easily tamed. Further along the coast, where there were low cliffs, there stood the ruins of a church, which had once served as a day-mark for sailors, but which was now falling into the sea, together with the cliff and the remains of the churchyard around it. The boy had been told that if you searched on the beach below, you might find pieces of the bodies which had earlier lain peacefully in the earth above. He had sometimes, fearfully, looked among the soft sand and

the sea wrack and once he had found a bone. It was a small bone, no longer than his fourth finger, washed and polished by the sea and the sand to a smooth whiteness. The boy had picked it up and wondered if he should take it home with him. Then he remembered a story he had heard at school of an old woman who had taken home a little bone, just like this, and who, in the night, had heard the steps and then the voice of the person to whom the bone had once belonged, coming to claim it back.

He left the bone among the rest of the flotsam on the shore.

He did not tell anyone about the bone. He told the old woman only what he had to, and she told him nothing except what she wanted him to do. They hardly talked to each other. If the boy asked her a question she did not want to answer, she

would not hear it. When he had been younger, he had sometimes asked, 'Have I got a Mum? Or a Dad? Have I ever had a Mum?' Once he had shouted in her ear, 'Is my Mum dead?'

The old woman did not look at him. She had busied herself at the kitchen sink.

The boy had shouted louder. 'You don't tell me anything! I want to know! Is my Mum dead?'

The old woman had heard this and she had hit him on the side of his head. It stung, but it did not really hurt. She still did not speak, and the boy soon stopped asking.

But he did not stop wondering. The children at his school belonged to families. Some of them had a Mum and some had a Dad and some had both. Many of them had brothers and sisters and aunts and uncles and grandmothers, too. Those children who, like him, did not live in families, came from a Children's Home the other side of the town, and they had someone called a House-mother and also a House-father, and they had each other. Of course they squabbled and quarrelled and fought, but most of them also had friends. The boy did not. He lived too far from the town to meet any of the children after school or at weekends. And, besides, he did not know how to make friends. As far as he could remember, he had never felt close to anyone, and he did not know now how to begin. No one teased or bullied him after he had learned to hit out quickly. The other children left him alone and he knew that they feared him a little and did not like him at all. They left him to himself, as much as they could, and this did not worry him, because he had never known anything else. He was used to being solitary, alone.

The old woman was not unkind to him. She cooked food

and put it before him. She cleaned the cottage and washed and mended his clothes. But nor was she kind. For the boy, it was as if he lived with a machine, which could supply his daily needs, but which knew and cared nothing of what he thought or felt. He supposed that when he had been a baby she must have dressed him and undressed him, put him to bed, perhaps held him in her arms. But he could not remember that time. He could not recall that she had ever touched him, unless she was angry and hit out at him. He and she seemed to live separate lives in the same house, as if there were an invisible wall between them which neither of them could penetrate.

'Write something about what you do in your spare time,' his teacher told the class. But when she read what the boy had written, she was not pleased.

'You can do better than this! What do you really do when you're out of school?' she asked.

'Nothing much,' the boy said.

'Haven't you any hobbies? You live by the sea, don't you? Do you go fishing?'

'No.'

'Do you swim?'

'No.'

'Don't you go in for sport with your friends?' she asked.

He didn't say that he hadn't any friends. He said, 'There's no one to go with, where I live.'

'I suppose you spend all your time watching the telly?' the teacher said, frowning.

'We don't have a telly.'

'What do you do, then?'

He did not want to tell her that he did the jobs around the house which the old woman found difficult. He said, 'I read.'

'What do you read?'

'Books,' the boy said, not meaning her to know. He had read all the old woman's books long ago. Now he went once a week to the school library and found for himself books which he thought looked interesting. Sometimes they were, often they were not. But still he went on reading. He did not ask for help from the school librarian, he was sure she would give him books he did not want to read. He did not trust anyone enough to ask for help.

'Next time, write me something about a book you've read,' the teacher said. But the boy did not mean to do this. He did not want to let her know what went on in his mind. He was a secret, a lonely boy. He was not unhappy, but he was not happy, either. He lived on the edge of other people's lives at school, in the town, among the few other cottages near his own. Sometimes he felt that he lived on the edge of the world.

II

It was on a cold, windy day in February, in the year of his tenth birthday, that he found the secret pool.

He was walking back from school in the afternoon, carrying the week's supplies of food from one of the small town's shops. He did this every Friday, now that the old woman no longer went out beyond the cottage garden. In his mind, the boy was going over the list she had made out for him and hoping that he had found the right brand of tinned meat she wanted and that the change would be correct. The plastic bag of groceries was heavy and he walked slowly. The road was deserted, there was nothing to hold his interest, only the dunes on his left and the flat, sedgy land with low bushes and small, wind-blown trees, to his right. He had not yet reached the post-office-shop and the duckpond, but he had not much further to go. He was hungry. He thought there might be baked beans on toast for his tea and he walked a little faster, looking forward to the warmth of the kitchen in the cottage.

Suddenly his eye caught a movement in the grass, and he saw a small animal jerking away from him among the tall stems. He thought it might be a stoat or a weasel; possibly one of the minks which had escaped from the mink farm some miles away and had run wild. He had got into trouble before now by forgetting to shut up the old woman's hens in the shed at night, and two birds had been lost to one or other of these small fierce animals. The boy wanted to get a clearer view of whatever it was, and he started after it. But it was impossible to move quietly with the plastic bag, it delayed his progress and the tins inside it rattled against each other. He put it under a bush just off the path, and followed the creature, which he could hear, moving in front of him.

It seemed to be teasing him. There would be a silence, then he would detect a rustling ahead of him. He expected every moment to catch up with it so as to be able to see it properly. That would be something he could put in his book next time the teacher told the class to write about something they had done or seen the week before. The boy had always disliked this exercise. He had nothing to say. Nothing ever happened to him. But next Monday he could write, 'I tracked a wild mink through the grass, I got right up to it.' Then he would describe how it looked. He knew that mink and stoat and weasels were vicious and must not be approached too close, otherwise he would have liked to imagine that he might capture it and take it home, tame it and keep it as a pet. But there was no chance of that, he must make do with a sighting.

Now he was among reeds instead of grass. They were tall, so tall that they reached his shoulder, and the ground under his feet was no longer hard and dry, but soft and marshy. The sharp wind from the sea stirred the reed stalks and they whispered and rustled, and he realised he had lost all sounds of the little animal's retreat. He had very little chance of finding it now. He was turning to go back to the road, when he caught sight of water, reflecting all the light there was from the huge grey sky overhead. He hadn't known there was a stream or a river here, and he pushed on to have a look at it before going back. Perhaps the little animal would be there, drinking, and he would see it after all.

He crept through the reeds, and, peering between their harsh stalks, he saw a pool. Quite a large pool fringed with reeds. As he watched, a small bird with a bobbing head, swam quickly across from one side to the other, followed by two or three more. Then they disappeared, and the pool lay deserted, its surface just flicked into motion by the teasing wind. The water barely moved where it met the mud at the edge where he stood. Silence surrounded it and the boy. He stood there for some time, waiting for the small birds to reappear, but they remained hidden.

'It is a secret pool! No one else knows that it's here. It's my secret pool,' he said to himself, hugging the discovery as something of his own.

He left it at last, and returned to the path by the road. Then he looked for the plastic bag which he had hidden under the bush. But it had gone. He searched around, though he knew exactly where he had left it. But it was not to be found. He grew desperate, and looked in the impossible places. Someone must have taken it. Not many cars used the road, but other people walked along it, and there were bicyclists. It was likely that one of these had seen the white bag, half hidden under the bush, and had dismounted to look. It wasn't surprising if someone had gone off with it. Plastic bags containing a week's supply of food, apparently unowned and deserted, are treasure trove, there for the taking. He should have hidden it more securely, but then he had not meant to be away for more than a

couple of minutes. It was his fault, and the old woman would know it.

When he reached the cottage, he had to explain that he had lost everything. And there was very little money to give back. He was not surprised that she was angry. She did not hit him, but she muttered and shouted, and by her indistinct words he understood that they were both going to suffer for what he had done. There was very little in the house left to eat, and it was going to be a hungry weekend. When she had calmed down a little, she gave him a piece of bread, with a smear of margarine on it, together with a mug of half-strength tea. She showed him, by signs, that what they had in the larder cupboard must be hoarded to last them over the weekend.

It was lucky, the boy thought, that it was Spring, and the hens were laying. He was hungry when he went to bed that night, and perhaps the old woman was hungry too, though she did not say so. He was kept awake for a time by the rumblings of his empty belly, but when he remembered the pool which he had discovered, he smiled and thought that the hunger was a small price to pay.

He was not so sure of this during the cold weekend. The old woman made a soda loaf and they lived on that and eggs and the end of a pot of jam. When the boy went back to school on Monday morning, he was hungry enough to look forward to the school dinner. From some hiding-place, the old woman had put together nearly two pounds in odd coins, and she gave this to the boy, with a list of what he was to buy at the store. He understood from her mumblings and her gestures what would happen to him if he failed to bring the goods back today. He had learned the lesson. He came straight home with a second plastic bag a quarter full, and that night the old woman cooked faggots and onion and potatoes. The boy could have eaten twice as much, but they still had to be sparing because of the goods he had lost.

The boy saw that the old woman gave him more than his fair share of the food, but he was still hungry. When he collected the eggs from the hens' shed, he was tempted always to keep one for himself, instead of taking them all in to the old woman. On the Thursday of that empty week, he yielded to the temptation. Just as he was leaving the shed, he saw that the brown and white speckled hen had not gone out into the

11

garden with the others to pick up the food he had scattered
there, but was squatting on a ledge, half hidden behind a pile
of empty boxes. The boy went near, meaning to shoo her out,
but she did not move, only looked at him with a stupid,
bright, frightened eye. Then he thought that perhaps she was
laying an egg. He slid his hand under her soft breast and his
fingers closed round the egg he had been hoping for. He did

not put it with the others, he felt that it was an extra; if he hadn't looked around for the speckled hen he would never have found it. He knew he was doing a mean thing, and that the old woman must be as hungry as he was, probably hungrier, for she did not get any school dinners. Then he thought that during the day when he was not there, she could help herself to all the food she wanted. He put the egg into his pocket. When he went in, he showed the five eggs in the bowl, and the old woman seemed satisfied. So he knew he was going to keep the egg to eat secretly that evening when she had gone to bed.

He came downstairs when he was sure the old woman would be asleep, with the egg in his hand. He never did any cooking, but he had seen the old woman boil eggs and now he copied what she did. He left the egg in the boiling water for ten minutes, and from the larder cupboard he stole a slice of bread and spread it with margarine. Then he took the egg out of the saucepan and cracked it. His mouth was full of hungry juices, and his belly stirred as he looked forward to this stolen night feast.

The shell fell apart. But he did not see the solid white that he expected. Instead, the limp body of a tiny naked chick fell half out of the shell, its head dangling on a thin scrawny neck.

It was horrible. It was disgusting. His insides heaved. He ran to the door and out into the garden, when he vomited.

He knew now why the speckled hen had hidden herself. Several times before this, the old woman had raised chicks, and the boy had liked seeing the small fluffy yellow chicks running about the yard. He had wished that chickens didn't have to grow up into stupid, graceless hens. Now he had killed one of those chicks. Instead of being alive and growing, it was a hideous *thing*, lying where he had left it on the kitchen table.

He could not make himself touch it with his fingers. He poked it onto the kitchen shovel and carried it out into the road. He threw it as far as he could over the ditch, into the field beyond. He went back into the cottage feeling cold and shaky. He felt as if he had murdered someone.

He did not think the old woman would find out what had happened. She could not know how many eggs the speckled hen was hatching, and when, a week later, four lively baby chicks were seen around her, the old woman did not complain that there should have been more. But every time the boy saw them, he felt a pang of guilt.

III

Between the cottage where the boy and the old woman lived, and the town where he went to school, there was a wide, flat expanse of water, a small estuary, where a little river ran down to meet the sea. Every day the boy trod the bridge that carried the road over the water, once in the morning on his way to school, once in the afternoon on his way back. Sometimes he stopped on the bridge to watch the water crawling sluggishly beneath his feet; sometimes he went down on to the grass bank and leant down to try to catch minnows in his hands. If he looked upstream from the bridge, he often saw fishermen, anglers, sitting with their rods and lines, their umbrellas and their baskets, at the point where the river ran deeper, and he thought how cold they must be and wondered whether they caught anything to make their vigil worthwhile.

After the occasion when he had lost the week's rations of food, it occured to him that perhaps he could catch something larger than a minnow, which would be a welcome addition to their diet. He had read in story-books that it was possible to catch fish with bait on a bent pin, a long stick and a length of string. But this Spring, when he looked up the river from the bridge, he did not see the usual line of anglers waiting patiently for a catch, and one afternoon, when the sun had a little more warmth than it had had for the last months, and the wind blew soft from the south, the boy walked up the river and round the bend which hid its upper reaches from the bridge, to find out where the anglers had gone, and to make up his mind where he himself should try to fish if he meant to make the attempt. There were trees here, and the river meandered in curves like a snake, flowing quietly over the flat ground, and sometimes expanding sideways into backwaters where the water was still and surrounded by rushes and reeds. These backwaters were not as secret and beautiful as the pool the boy had discovered the month before, but they did have something that his pool had not. He had turned aside to look more closely at one of them, and was just about to leave, finding the main river more interesting, when there was a movement on the further side of the water, and out from the reeds came a pair of swans. They swam so smoothly that they seemed to glide, as if they were propelled by magic. Their great white bodies floated on the surface of the pool and were reflected below them, so that each swan seemed to have another, an exact double, swimming upside down beneath it. They came out to the middle of the pond, side by side, a royal couple, sometimes dipping their long elegant necks down into the water, so that they left only their bodies, like two vast feathered eggs, in sight.

At school, the boy had seen a video film about swans. It had shown a couple swimming side by side, preening each other's plumage like this. It had shown the swans building a nest, raising their young. It had also shown the fate of swans which had been choked by the hooks of anglers and poisoned by the lead weights used at the end of the fishing line. It had been a

sad film in some ways, but the boy had seen people who spent their time trying to rescue the swans from the dangers that threatened them. He hadn't taken very much notice of the video at the time, but now that he saw these birds close to, for himself, he knew that he hated the fishermen whose carelessness was killing grand creatures like this couple. As he gazed now, the swans raised their heads from the water, turned towards each other, and each, with its bill, groomed the feathers of the other. The boy saw that this was a courtship. The pair were caressing each other.

The boy knew, for the first time in his life, that what he was looking at was beautiful. Something inside his chest hurt and turned over and his throat was tight. He was angry with himself. It was stupid to have feelings like this, just about a couple of big birds.

But he stayed, watching them, for a long time. He watched them searching for food at the bottom of the pond. He watched them swim away and back again. He saw one swan go out onto the muddy edge of the pond, walking with an ungainly, flat-footed gait which did not suit its majestic progress on water. Presently the other swan followed into the reeds, and then the boy remembered that he was supposed to be on his way home, and he went quickly back to the bridge and the road, and ran part of the way back so that the old woman should not scold him.

After this, he went often up the river to the little backwater. He liked watching the swans. He had given up his intention to fish, and there were no other anglers to remind him. He spent as long as he could, crouching or lying among the reeds, watching the swans. There was only one pair, he discovered, on this particular stretch of the river. He wished they had been on his secret pool; that would have made them more especially his own. But because he never saw anyone else in the backwater, he began to believe that no one but he had ever visited it, and that no one else knew about this one pair. There were plenty of other swans on other reaches of the estuary, but this couple were separate from the others, just as he was separate from the other children in his school. If he had known what the word meant, he might have said that he loved the swans.

When he had been watching them for nearly a month, he went to the teacher who looked after the school library.

'I want a book about birds,' he said, careful not to mention the word 'swan' in case someone discovered his secret.

She was surprised. This boy had never asked her for a book before.

'What sort of book? A story book? Or an information book?'

'I want a book that tells about what birds do.'

'You mean their habits and habitat?'

He did not understand the word 'habitat', and she explained. 'Where they live and build their nests. What sort of country you'd find them in.'

He agreed, and she gave him a book called *British Birds*. It was full of coloured pictures and he was surprised to find how many birds he knew by sight, though he had known the names of only a few. Sparrow. Blackbird. Robin. But the book told him that he had also seen swallows and martins and fieldfares and blue tits and kestrels and others which spent the winter in the bleak country where he lived because it was less cold than the far north from which they came. He was pleased by this, but disappointed in what he found about swans. Two paragraphs described the rivers and ponds where swans were to be found, their eating and nesting habits, their plumage, their flight. The picture of the swan was boring, flat. It didn't give the impression it should have of the silver majesty of his swans. He took the book back to the library without enthusiasm.

'Interesting?' the teacher asked him, as he handed her the volume.

He lied. 'Yes.' Then, needing to know more, he asked, 'What does "mute" mean?'

'Mute?' she asked, puzzled.

'It says "The Mute Swan".'

'Oh, yes. Means it doesn't sing. It hasn't a proper song like other birds. Not like . . . a blackbird. Or a nightingale.'

'You mean it's dumb?' He was disappointed.

'They say it sings just once, when it's going to die. Right at the end.'

The boy was enthralled. This was magic. He imagined those lovely creatures lifting their long curved necks and opening their powerful throats to let out a song such as no other bird could ever achieve. He did not know what it would be like, but because the swan is such a large bird, he thought it would be more startling and more brilliant than any bird-song in the world. And if you sing only once in your life, it must surely be a very special last song?

'Anything else?' the librarian was asking him.

He said, 'No,' then remembered something else that had puzzled him. 'It says in the book that swans mate for life. What does that mean?'

'What it says. They stay as one pair. Husband and wife. They don't change. They stay . . . married . . . to each other till they die.'

The boy thought about this too. On his way home that after-noon, he wondered what happened if one of the swan pair died. Could the one that was left find another mate? But he did not ask any more. He did not like asking questions, he pre-ferred to wait until he could find things out for himself. But he was troubled by the idea of a single lonely swan. He went up the river then to look at his swans, to make sure that they were there, safely together. He saw them floating serenely on the water, their reflections bright in the afternoon Spring sun. He was comforted. They were together. All was well.

IV

During the next weeks, he noticed a change in the behaviour of the swan pair. They spent more time on the muddy bank among the reeds and less on the water. It took him a little time to understand, then one day, when he was observing them, he knew what was happening. They were building a nest.

The next time he visited them, he went round to the further side of the backwater and crept through the reeds. And there he saw the nest, an untidy sprawl of twigs and weed, flat on the marshy ground. The female was re-arranging some part of it, and as he looked, the male bird came walking awkwardly towards her, with weed in its beak, which it added to the heap. Then they changed places, the female went off to gather more materials for the nest. There were no eggs in it as yet. But the boy was glad. He had liked the idea that these swans mated for life. Now he wanted to see them with baby swans. Cygnets, they were called, he had learned from the boring book.

This was a Thursday. He would not be able to go up the river the next day. After school he must go to the shop and he dared not risk losing their supplies of food again. Nor would he be able to go during the weekend. That was when the old woman made him do the work around the house that she was

22

no longer capable of. He would have to clean out the hens'
shed, weed the potato patch, clean his room and the kitchen.
Unless the old woman slept on the Sunday afternoon, he
would have very little time for himself.

On the Friday morning he went again to the school library,
and this time he asked for a book about swans. If the librarian
asked why, he was not going to tell her of the pair he watched
in case she talked to anyone else who might want to seek them

out. He could pretend that his interest arose from the video his class had been shown.

'Swans? We haven't any books about swans,' the librarian said.

'There must be something,' the boy said.

'Not books. There are fairy stories. There's Elsa and the seven swans.'

The boy did not want a fairy story. He did not want to hear about Elsa.

'You did have that book about birds,' the librarian said.

'I want a book that's just about swans.'

'There might be one in that set of little books.'

The boy knew the little books and he despised them. They were written for little kids who had only just learned to read. He went to the shelves and looked for himself. He even looked among the story books, but they were about cops and robbers or smugglers and pirates or about families. At another time he might have chosen a book of adventure, but now he did not even open one. He wanted to read about swans. He was not interested in anything else.

He spent some time searching the shelves. Books on hobbies. He didn't have any. Books on history. History bored him. Books on cars and aeroplanes, books on computers, books on photography and on woodwork. He did look at books on animals, but they seemed to be about monkeys and tigers, mice, dogs, cats, budgerigars. He was disconsolate. Did no one write about swans?

He had given up hope and was on his way out of the library, when his eye was caught by the picture on the jacket of one of the books lying on the display table near the librarian's desk. He stopped. The picture showed a swan sailing on the water towards him. On her head she wore a gold crown. She was stately, like a queen or a princess. He looked at the title. SWAN LAKE.

He picked the volume up and looked inside. There were more pictures, some drawn in black and white, some painted. Several were photographs. There were more swans, there were also girls, women standing in front of a pool or lake, surrounded by trees and reeds, just like the pools and backwaters he knew. The girls wore full white skirts, and in some of the pictures they were dancing.

He took the book to the librarian.

'I'll take this.'

She was doubtful. 'That isn't a book about birds.'

'It's called Swan Lake,' he said.

'It's just a story. It's a bally.'

He did not know what a bally was. 'I want it,' he said, and took it away.

At home that evening, he hid the book till he was in bed. Like the pool and the swan pair, it had to remain a secret.

That night, he read. He did not trouble himself to read the long introduction, which was about a composer whose name he could not read properly, and about a theatre in Russia and a lot of dancers. What interested him was the story, which began when the pictures began. He read it all, straight through.

There was a prince. That was usual in the stories which had been read to him when he was small, at school. But this prince did not set out to seek his fortune or to kill a monster, or to prove that he was the best of the King's sons in order to inherit the kingdom. This prince wandered out into the country, just as the boy himself had wandered. The prince found a

25

secret lake, just as he had found the pool. The prince saw swans swimming on the lake and he hid himself among the reeds and watched them, as the boy had watched his swan pair. The prince had come there with a bow and arrows, meaning to shoot something. Did people really shoot swans? Why?

But the prince never shot his swan. Instead, as he watched from the reed bed, he saw the swans come to shore, where they turned into beautiful girls, who danced with each other on the lake's edge. The most beautiful was a princess, who wore a golden crown on her dark hair. There were photographs of both the swimming swans and of the girls, in long, full white skirts, dancing on the grass. The princess danced with the prince. That was right and fitting.

The boy read further, but the story became confusing to him. There was a wicked magician, who had enchanted the girls and turned them into swans. When he appeared, the girls became swans again and swam away over the lake, leaving the prince disconsolate. Then there was more confusion, with a wicked magician and another princess who looked like the swan-girl, but wasn't her. The boy skipped this and turned to the end, where the prince killed the magician and married the real princess, now no longer enchanted into a swan's shape, but a girl again.

The boy did not believe in wicked magicians. But he was puzzled by the book's illustrations. The photographs were of real swans and real girls. If the story were not a little true, how could anyone have taken photographs of it? The upper, sensible part of his brain knew quite well that swans do not turn into girls or girls into swans, and yet right at the back of his mind there was a longing that this sort of thing might happen; it would not be exactly as the book told the story, but there might be some mystery about swans which he didn't know about, some connection with dark-haired girls in long white dresses, who danced on the river-banks as beautifully as the swans floated on the water.

He went, as often as he dared, to the estuary to watch the swan pair. The female bird, the pen, was sitting on the nest now, she hardly moved from it. The boy saw the cob bring food for her in his beak and very occasionally it would be he who would guard the nest. During the weeks at the end of May and the beginning of June, the cold wind from the sea and the grey sky had suddenly changed and it was summer. The air was warm, the daylight lasted till it was time for the boy to go to bed. Birds sang. One day, as he was going to school, the boy stopped to listen to a blackbird which he could see on the branch of a tree in the hedge. It seemed to be beginning a tune which the boy felt he should recognise, but the tune did not finish, it remained four, six, eight notes of piercing beauty. The boy thought of his swans. Ah, when they sang their last song, it would be different! But he could not wish to hear the melody which would herald their deaths.

That evening, when he went to the estuary, the pen was sitting on the nest, but the cob was nowhere in sight. The boy crept towards her, excited but frightened, in case the male should think him an enemy and attack him. He did not like to go close; he crouched, motionless as a wild animal, about ten feet from the brooding bird, among the reeds. Presently, she turned her head and looked directly at him, and he knew that she knew that he was there. She did not move, she did not hiss to drive him away, she showed no sign of fear. The boy thought that she knew he meant her no harm. She trusted him. He was glad.

V

May came to an end and June began. The boy knew from the book he had read that the eggs would take from six to eight weeks to hatch out. He was excited. He couldn't wait to see the young cygnets.

One day, soon after midsummer, on a hot, still day, with the sky cloudless and dazzling above, he thought that the female, sitting on the nest, looked different. Her long neck drooped. Her feathers were not smooth, but rough, ungroomed. She was alert, but when she looked around she seemed to be anxious, as if she were searching for her mate. During the half hour the boy spent by the water's edge, on his way back from school, he did not see the male bird once.

But 'they mate for life', he thought. The cob would never have deserted the pen now, just when the eggs must be about to hatch.

He did not see the cob on the next day either, but this time he was sure there was something wrong with the pen. She no longer looked around her, but sat, almost lay, across the untidy nest. He could see her laboured breaths from where he crouched among the reeds.

On the third day, the boy found the body of the dead cob swan on the bank, a little further upstream than he usually went. It lay with its wings outstretched, a huge bird, magnificent in death, though its plumage was no longer white and its body had already been attached by scavengers which were still alive and hungry. The boy was both frightened and revolted by the sight. He did not want to go near the huge carcass. He left it lying on the sedge and went back to look again at the female on the nest. He was sure that she, too, was dying. Her eyes were half closed, she hardly moved. She was slumped forward, her neck supported on her breast. She did not appear to have noticed him, though he was closer to her than he had ever been. He stood for a long time, looking at her, wishing there was something he could do to help. He thought, 'They mate for life. She will die of a broken heart.'

When he got back to the cottage, the old woman was cross because he was late. She grumbled at him as she moved about the kitchen, but the boy took no notice. His heart was full of sorrow for the dying swan.

The next day was a Friday. He would not be able to go to look at the swan till the next day or Sunday, possibly not even then. This weekend, as usual, he would have to work hard round the house. The boy cleaned out the hens' shed, he dug the potatoes and mended a falling piece of fence between the garden of his cottage and the garden next door, which belonged to Mrs Dix, the neighbour who collected the old woman's pension money for her every week, and who sometimes took the boy into the town to get him new clothes. It wasn't until Sunday afternoon that the boy was able to leave the old woman half asleep in her chair, and to walk along the road to the estuary.

The fishermen were back today. More than a week ago, when the season had started, the banks of the river had been lined with their patient figures. He turned towards the backwater. The boy approached the nest carefully, fearing what he might find. He saw the swan on the nest, and saw that she was moving, and his heart lifted, believing that all was well. But as he came nearer, he saw that she was struggling. She twisted her neck this way and that. She half lifted herself off the ground, then fell back. The boy saw that her eyes were glazed and her plumage, dirty and disordered. He thought, 'She is dying now. In a minute she will sing her last song.' He so much wanted to hear that lovely death song, that he almost forgot to grieve. But the swan did not lift her head and sing. Instead, she struggled, half spreading her great wings, and drawing painful, gasping breaths. Then she leant forward, further, further, her wings still spread, until her head touched the ground and stayed there, motionless. The boy could no longer see her breath come and go.

He watched her lie, splayed out over the nest for five . . . ten minutes. Then he knew that he had seen her die.

There had been no song. The swan had died and had not sung her last and only song. The boy felt cheated.

He stood for a long time, looking at the dead bird.

He knew what he must do, but he did not want to do it. He did not like to go near to that large, lifeless bulk. He thought, 'Suppose she's not really quite dead, she might attack me.' And if she were really dead, he did not want to touch her body. He turned to leave the inlet, to walk away. Then he stopped and turned back.

He remembered the dead chick in the egg he had boiled, the egg he had stolen from under the speckled hen. Under the dead swan there must be eggs now. He knew that they would still be warm, and he thought, too, that they must be near to hatching out. There must be baby birds inside them, alive. If he left them now, they would grow cold as their mother's body cooled, and they, too, would die. They might die from the cold, or, more likely, some animal, like the mink he had seen near his secret pool, would come and steal the eggs and eat the babies inside them.

He hated going near the nest, but he knew that if he did not try to rescue one of those unborn baby birds, he would despise himself for the rest of his life. He had killed one shell-bound baby, but that had been a mistake. If he let these cygnets die, it would not be an accident. It would be deliberate murder.

At last, trembling, he crept towards the dead swan on the nest. He made as much noise as he could as he went, hoping, hoping that the swan would lift her head and look at him, proving that she was, after all, alive. Then he would be able to go away again and leave her to look after her own young. But she did not stir. He came up close, and he hesitated before he dared touch the bird. She was spread-eagled right over the nest. He had to push a wing aside. His stomach turned over, he tried not to think or feel. He put a hand under her breast, and somehow that was not so bad, it was almost comforting. Warm and soft. His fingers felt a smooth, rounded hard shape, also warm. An egg.

It was larger than he had expected. He had to stoop right down and use both hands to pull it out.

It was enormous. The largest egg he had ever seen or held. It was much paler than a hen's egg, greenish-white, speckled. Heavy.

There must be other eggs in the nest, but he could not carry more than one. He did not know what he was going to do with this one. He wanted to get away from this place, from the

dead swans. Holding the egg carefully in both hands, he
backed away from the inlet and returned to the road.

   He must somehow keep the egg warm. To his frightened
fancy, he could feel it cooling already. He unbuttoned the
front of his shirt and put the egg inside it, next to his skin,
above the belt of his pants, but in case that was not enough to
support it, he steadied it as he walked back, with one hand.
He hoped that none of the drivers on the road — and there
were not many — would notice the abrupt swelling of his
clothing. He thought, 'I am like the mother swan. I am

hatching her egg for her. I might have a swan to keep, of my own.'

He thought of the swan princess in the book. With most of his mind, he knew that swans do not turn into beautiful princesses. But his dreams were stronger at this moment, than his sense of what happens in the real world, and as he walked home, he imagined that the egg broke and that he would rear the baby swan until it became a large, beautiful, silver-white swan like its mother. In his mind's eye, he saw it gliding across a lake, he saw it dropping its swan feathers on the shore and dancing off, a girl in a white dress. He stole the feather-dress and she remained with him for ever. A wife? A mother? Someone who belonged to him, someone of his very own.

He knew it would never happen. But his dream went on.

When he got back to the cottage, the boy took the egg up to his room. He wrapped it in his thickest pullover, then his winter coat. He put it under the pillow on his bed, then he went downstairs to make tea for the old woman, to feed the hens, sweep out the kitchen, pretend that this was an ordinary day. But his mind was all the time with the swans, with the warm egg in his bed, by a lake in an enchanted land. After the old woman had climbed the stairs, painfully, to her bedroom, the boy fetched the egg and put it again under his shirt. Before going to sleep he laid the egg in his bed, not too near him, separated by a twist of garments so that he would not crush it in his sleep. But he slept fitfully, waking every hour to put out a hand to feel the egg. When his fingers told him that it was whole and warm, he could fall asleep again for another short spell.

The next day was Monday and he should go to school. But he did not dare to leave the egg in case it lost too much heat.

He made signs to the old woman that he had a sore throat and that his head hurt. She did not seem to be much interested. She told him to go back to bed. and for all that summer's day the boy lay in his bed, keeping the egg warm. He wondered how long he could pretend to be ill so that he could keep guard over it.

He stayed at home on the following day, the Tuesday, and was bored. He had read every book in the cottage. He could not go out because he was supposed to be ill. He lay on his bed, beside the large egg, which was wrapped in a blanket, sometimes putting his hand under the covering to make sure that it was warm enough. He was half asleep in the middle of the afternoon, when his fingers felt something different. The egg was sticky. His forefinger traced a crack. He took off the blanket and saw a hole, two, three holes in the shell. Something inside was moving. He tried to enlarge the holes with his fingernails, but they were not strong enough. He went downstairs and fetched a knife, then thought that too sharp and took a teaspoon instead. With the handle of the spoon he carefully chipped away the shell round the edge of the largest hole. There was a sound, a squawk. He could see the top of a downy head. He got two fingers inside the hole and pulled.

Five minutes later, he was looking at a cygnet, covered in greyish-brown down, asking in a loud, hungry voice, for food.

He must take it to water. He knew from the book on birds that young cygnets can feed themselves as soon as they are hatched. But they must have water. The boy hid the little bird inside his shirt and crept downstairs. Lucky that the old woman was asleep in her chair. Lucky, for once, that she was deaf and had not heard the baby bird's cries. The boy left the cottage and made for his secret pool.

The bird struggled against his chest, but he did not mind. The egg had hatched and the bird was alive. The first event of his daydream had come true.

When he reached the secret pool, he put the awkward, squawking thing down on the mud-bank. It took an uncertain step forward, then leant its small breast on the water and, miraculously, swam. The boy watched it, astonished. It seemed to know, without teaching, that it must stay near the edge of the pool, where the water was shallow, so that it could dip down to the bottom to feed. The moorhens and coots took no notice of the stranger. They were busy with their own young.

He stayed by the pool until his stomach told him that it was near to supper-time. When he got back, with the bird hidden in his shirt as before, he had to tell the old woman that he had felt better and gone for a walk. That meant that he must go to school tomorrow. And he must find some way of keeping the cygnet hidden and safe for the night.

After he and the old woman had eaten, he went out to the hens' shed, and fetched one of the empty wooden boxes which had been stacked there ever since he could remember. He took it up to his room and lined it with paper, torn from one of his school exercise books. He put the baby bird in the box. Then he added a pair of old socks.

The cygnet did not seem happy. It moved restlessly about the box and uttered small, squeaking noises. The boy thought, 'If it was night, it would sleep under its mother. It wouldn't feed all night.' He took a blanket off his bed and covered the box. Then he sat by it, waiting. The noises continued for a short time, then there was silence. Very cautiously, the boy lifted the blanket and looked. The cygnet was quiet, its eyes shut.

That night he slept even worse than when he had had the egg in bed with him. He got up several times to listen, but he heard nothing. When it was light, early, because it was July, he took off the blanket. He feared that he might find the bird dead. But it woke immediately and asked to be fed. The boy crept out of the cottage and carried it to the pool, his footsteps leaving green marks on the dew-white grass. The cygnet floated away from him on the water and he saw that it was picking up weed from the shallows. The morning was cold and he was shivering, but he was also triumphant. The bird had been out of its shell and alive for twelve whole hours.

He decided not to go back to school. There were only another five days before the end of the summer term, the rest of this week and two days in the next. If he didn't go back at all, no one would ask him for a note to say why he had been away, and by the autumn they might have forgotten. Or he would think up some good excuse. All he had to do was to go off in the morning as usual and to get back not too early in the afternoon, so that the old woman would believe that he was in school. So, on the Wednesday and Thursday of that week, he went out after breakfast, with his school bag on his shoulder and the cygnet against his chest. He had to spend the whole day by the pool, watching the bird feed. He stole food from the cottage food cupboard, but he dared not take much in case the old woman discovered the theft, and for most of the day he was hungry. Fortunately the weather was not bad; when it rained he was wet, his old waterproof could not keep all of him dry, but it was never cold. He had nothing to read for the first two days, but on the Friday he had to go to the village in order to do the customary week's shopping. He dared not leave the cygnet in the pool by itself for fear of predators, so he carried it under his shirt to and from the village. For part of the time it slept, but when it was awake it cried, and he was grateful when he could let it out in the pool on his way back. He had bought himself a couple of paperbacks from the market stall, too, so the weekend passed more easily for him. For two days the next week he again pretended to go to school, but after the Tuesday there was no longer any need for pretence, and he could take a more substantial midday meal with him when he went out. He spent every day by the side of the secret pool, watching the cygnet, watching the moorhens, listening to the skylarks whose trills were as fast as the beating wings that held them up in the air above him. He saw kestrels and sparrowhawks too; if they came close, he stood up and clapped his hands to scare them off. He kept his eyes open for another mink or a ferret or skunk which might be a danger to his bird. He tried to be as watchful as the parent swans would have been. Every evening, he carried it back and covered it up in its box. And it grew. It was already much larger than a chick of the same age, and as the summer wore on, its brownish down was beginning to give way to feathers. For all that, it was still a baby. The boy had found that he could call it to him with the low whistle of three notes on the rising scale. When he held it under his shirt, it nestled against his skin as it might have nestled against its mother's feathered breast. The boy thought 'It feels my heart beating, and it knows it is safe with me.'

Lying still among the reeds for hours at a time, the boy saw things he had never known of. He saw water-rats, voles; he watched spiders spin their intricate webs between the tall stems of reeds and grasses. Once he saw a snake coil its way along the muddy ground. He saw toads and frogs, water-boatmen, dragonflies. On one of his weekly visits to the town, he bought himself a new, empty notebook, and in it he wrote, laboriously, everything he saw. He even tried to draw, but what came out on the paper was so different from the real thing, that he was disgusted, and tore the pages out. Words were better. Sometimes he slept on the sun-hardened mud, then woke, fearful that his lack of care might have enabled an enemy to seize his cygnet. But he was fortunate. Each time he started awake, the cygnet was circling the pool, feeding; or if he did not catch sight of it at once, the whistled notes would summon it from behind a patch of reeds, and he would breathe freely again.

About halfway through the holiday, he noticed that there was a difference in the old woman since the summer before. Then, when he had been off school, she had given him daily jobs to do, she had wanted to know where he was going if he left the cottage. She had been more active in body, more alert in mind. This month of August, in spite of the heat, she hardly ever went out. She spent most of the day sitting in her chair, more often than not dozing, snoring, often grunting as if she were carrying on a conversation with herself. The food she told the boy to buy on Fridays was now generally in tins or packets. She hardly cooked at all, except to make tea and occasionally to scramble the eggs he collected from the hens. The neighbour, Mrs Dix, coming in with the old woman's pension money, wrinkled up her nose and told the boy he should clean the kitchen, his Gran wasn't up to it. The boy tried to do as she had said. After he had swept the floor, which was his usual task, he got a bucket of water and began to wash the slates with an old, balding mop. But the old woman made signs to him to stop, and he understood that she was frightened of slipping on the wet surface. He made a sort of effort at cleaning his own room, but he did not attempt to do anything in the old woman's. When the door was open, a sour, stuffy smell came from it, but the old woman never let him inside. He could do nothing about it.

He noticed too that the old woman had become clumsy. Her hand, holding the knife, shook as she peeled potatoes and she sometimes cut herself. She walked more and more slowly, and she had difficulty in getting up from her chair, as well as in letting herself down to sit. One day, she asked the boy, in her strange language, and with signs, to find her a stick. He looked around in the hedges for the straight branch of a tree or a bush, but it was a long time before he found one that was straight and stout enough. He had to borrow a saw from Mr Dix in order to hack it off the tree, and it took him more than two weeks of hard work by the pool to strip off the bark and to smooth it with the wire wool with which the old woman had formerly scoured saucepans. When he had finished, and he could see the grain of the wood, he polished it with floor-wax and was astonished at what he had done. He had made something good, something handsome. It was the first time he had ever admired his own work.

The old woman took the stick without thanks. But she used it constantly. The boy was surprised to find that because he had spent time working on it, he felt for the old woman something like a very pale shadow of the protective pity he felt for the little bird he was caring for. Not love. Love would

be too strong a word. But it was a new feeling that he had
never had for her before. It did not last. After a couple of days
it had gone, and they were back again in the shared loneliness
in which they had always lived together.

VI

The boy knew that when the Autumn school term began, he would have to leave the cygnet for the larger part of the day. The thought worried him. The bird was at risk on the secret pool, there were too many enemies around, and the busy, head-bobbing moorhens would not protect it. After turning over many different, impossible, plans in his head, he decided that the safest thing to do would be to leave the cygnet every morning on the duckpond down the road, near the post office. There were often people passing by, which must mean that there was less likelihood of predators. Besides, the number of other birds on the pond would lessen the danger for any one. It was not a perfect solution, but it was the best he could think of. So one morning in September, he set off for school five minutes early, with his school bag over his shoulder and the cygnet beneath his pullover and raincoat. He hated leaving it on the pond. Compared with the pool surrounded by rushes and reeds, the pond seemed so small, so bare and also so over-crowded. But he had reckoned on there being safety in numbers. He put the small creature down on the concrete slope that led into the water, and watched it straddle down and launch itself, confidently among the other birds. Then the boy walked on along the road towards the town. He looked back often, but all he saw was the empty road stretching away behind him.

He had no attention for his teachers that day. His mind was always on the cygnet, on the pond, on all the dangers which he hadn't imagined before. Suppose the bird left the pond and wandered out on to the road? It would be killed by a van, a car. It had no experience of traffic. Suppose someone passing saw that it did not belong to the families of ducks and geese, and stole it? What if the ducks and geese turned on it as a stranger and attacked? When it was time for him to go home, he ran along the last half mile of the road leading to the pond. When he was there, he looked with eyes so anxious that they could not distinguish the object of his search. But then he saw it, the dusky brown bird with the longer neck than a duck. He felt heavy with relief. He crouched on the edge of the pond and whistled, and at once the cygnet paddled towards him. It was dripping as he hauled it out of the water, and before he was back at the cottage, all his clothes were soaked. As he put the bird into its box, he stroked its feathers, he held it up to his face and felt the warm softness of its breast on his cheek. He was giddy with triumph. He covered the box with the blanket, changed into old dry jeans and went down to his tea. The old woman did not appear to have noticed anything strange about his homecoming. She did not ask him about his first day back at school. The evening was silent, but the boy was happy.

That term, for the first time, the boy was not at a loss when the teacher told the class to write about something they had done during the holiday. He copied some of the notes he had made during those long, lonely days watching by the pool. He was astonished to find how easy it was to write when he had things he wanted to tell. The teacher read a part of his composition aloud to the class. Afterwards, she said to him, 'Very good! I didn't know you could write like that. You must go on and write some more.'

The boy had not known that he could write, either. But now that he had done it once, he could do it again. If he had his cygnet to write about.

After this, he left the cygnet on the duck-pond every morning as he went to school and evey afternoon he collected the bird again on his way home. By November he had to carry it in a plastic bag. It was too large to be hidden inside his clothes. When the Christmas holidays came, he changed the routine and took the bird to the pool instead, and now that it was so much bigger, he dared to leave it there for an hour or two, alone, with no one to guard it. It was just as well that he could do this, for that Spring term the old woman had an accident, and the course of the boy's life changed for ever.

He came back one Sunday from a cold watch by the pool, to find her lying on the floor, groaning. She had tripped on the stairs and fallen. After he had left the cygnet in its box in his room, he ran to the callbox outside the post-office at the crossroads, and rang the emergency service. He asked, in a breathless whisper for an ambulance. 'It's my Gran. She's fallen downstairs and she's hurt,' he said, and gave his name and the address. The ambulance arrived half an hour later. Two men, ready with comforting talk which somehow did not reassure the boy, lifted the old woman on to a stretcher and took her into the back of their van.

'You'd better come along too,' one of them said to the boy.

'Where? Where're you taking her?' he asked.

'Hospital. You can't stay here on your own.'

If he let them take him to the hospital, which was in the town, how would he ever get back? What would happen to the cygnet, trustfully asleep upstairs? 'I can't come,' he said.

'You can't stop on here by yourself,' the man repeated.

'I'll be all right. There's Mrs Dix next door. She'll see to me,' he lied.

'You sure? I'd better just find out,' the man said.

The boy had known that Mrs Dix was not at home. When the man returned from his useless knocking at her door, he repeated, 'She's looked after me before. I'll be all right.'

The ambulance man was not happy about leaving the boy alone. But he had to get the groaning old woman to hospital and he did not want to lose time. He said, 'Well! I hope it's all right.' Then he and his assistant drove off along the straight, empty road towards the town, and the boy was left in the cold cottage to look after himself.

The next day, early, before he had gone out, a small car drove up to the cottage door. A young woman got out and came to the door of the kitchen, where the boy was getting his breakfast.

'Are you the boy whose Gran's gone to hospital?' she asked.

'Yes.'

'I'm a social worker. Your social worker.' She smiled at him, but he did not know what she meant, when she said she was 'his'.

'Someone has to look after you, now your Gran's not here,' she said.

'I don't need looking after. I'm all right,' the boy said, as he had said to the ambulance man the day before.

'I'm afraid you aren't allowed to stay here on your own. It's against the law,' the young woman said.

45

The boy knew nothing about the law.

'Can I come in?' the young woman said. She came into the kitchen and sat on a chair.

'Would you like some tea?' the boy asked. He knew that when you had a visitor, you should offer tea.

The young woman accepted the cup of tea. While the kettle of water was boiling, she said, 'I'm very sorry to have to take you away, but I haven't any choice. We aren't allowed to leave children living alone.'

'I'm managing all right,' the boy said.

'How old are you?' the young woman asked.

'I'm thirteen,' he lied. He saw the doubt on her face and said, 'I'm small for my age.'

'You'd have to be older than that to be let live alone,' she said. She took the mug of tea and thanked him. The boy watched the way she held the mug in the tips of her fingers. He listened to her voice, which was different from the voices he was used to. He thought that he liked her small, clear face, and he liked her straight, mousey hair. He liked the way she talked to him, because she did not patronise him, she spoke instead as if he and she were the same age.

'When someone your age is left alone, like you are, the law says that the social services are to look after you. To see that you are safe and have a place to live. It's part of my job to see to you now. I have to take you back to the town and find a place where you can stay till your Gran is well enough to come home,' she said.

'There's Mrs Dix next door,' the boy said.

'I'm afraid that won't do. I'm sorry. I know you'd rather stay here. But I have to do my job. You see?' she asked him.

'Do I have to go now?' the boy asked. He was thinking of the cygnet, in the box upstairs.

'Do you need time to pack up?' the young woman asked.

'Yes. I have to pack,' the boy said.

The young woman got up from the table.

'I could come back and fetch you this afternoon. That would give me a chance to try to find somewhere for you.'

'I'll be ready this afternoon,' the boy said.

'You won't run away? You'll be here when I come back? About four o'clock?' she said.

'I'll be here.'

'You promise?'

The boy promised. He was not sure that he would keep his promise, but he had to get rid of the young woman while he thought what to do with the cygnet.

VII

He watched the little car drive away. Then he fetched the sleepy bird and carried it out to the pool. It was cold out on the sedge, and he had things he wanted to do in the cottage, so he left the cygnet feeding. He would go back in the middle of the day, when he had made his preparations. First he packed a few clothes in a plastic bag. Then he collected the food from the larder cupboard and put it with the clothes. He had to get away. He would have to go far away, so that the young social worker would not be able to find him. For this, he would need money. He knew that the old woman had kept a store of money somewhere. Now he was going to find it.

In the half light of a grey February day, he searched the cottage. He looked first in the kitchen dresser, but there was nothing there but cracked china and old bent kitchen cutlery, a rolling-pin which he had never seen used, and a block of writing-paper with pictures of flowers at the top of each blank page. He went upstairs to the old woman's bedroom and looked through the cupboard and the chest of drawers. The cupboard had nothing but the old woman's clothes, rusty, patched, threadbare. The boy remembered that he had never seen her wear anything new.

In the two small top drawers of the chest, there were

packets of envelopes and papers. The stamps on the envelopes were unfamiliar colours, long out of date. He shook out the contents and saw letters, written in an unfamiliar sloping hand, the ink so faded that he could not read the words in the poor light. But one long, brown envelope held something different. It was a document or form, partly printed, partly written in by hand. He puzzled over it for some time before he realised that it was something to do with a marriage, years and years ago. The date was nineteen-thirty, and one of the names he read was familiar. Aishe. That was his name, and it had been the name of the old woman. He was surprised at the name Violet. Had the old woman really had a name like that? No. This Violet Aishe had married Walter Bridwell. Who was he? What had this marriage form to do with him? He had never heard the name Bridwell.

He stared at the piece of paper for a long time, then he went on with his search. Another envelope, which crumbled into shreds as he touched it, contained a brown sepia photograph on hard board, of a family. The parents sat in the middle, six children of different ages, wearing odd, old-fashioned clothes, stood around them. Their small pale faces stared back at him from the print, blank, unknown, telling him nothing. The girls had long hair scraped back from their foreheads, the boys wore knickerbockers and stiff white collars. The boy of today looked at those blank eyes and mouths and wondered what this had to do with him? He could not tell why the old woman had kept this photograph. Had she been one of the long-haired girls?

Next, he found an old leather purse. Here was the old woman's treasure. There were out-of-date pound notes, three five-pound notes which he recognised as useful, and several coins. He put the purse in his pocket. This might be his pass to freedom.

He found other envelopes containing papers, which he did not try to read. And at the bottom of the pile, another photograph. A snapshot, this time, small and not very clear. It showed a girl, who could have been any age between fifteen and twenty, standing against the side of a house where a rose grew up on a trellis. The girl wore a white dress with a full skirt. Her long dark hair hung over her shoulders, nearly down to her waist. Her hands were lightly clasped in front of her body and she was looking at the camera with a smile which had narrowed her eyes but had not yet reached her lips. Her head was slightly on one side; she looked as if she were teasing the person behind the camera. The boy turned the paper over and saw, written on the back, one name only. 'Jennie'.

He was studying it, when he heard the sound of a car engine in the road. He put the photograph of the dark-haired girl into an envelope and hid it under his shirt. He pushed all the other papers back into the drawer and went quickly downstairs. Beyond the garden gate, he saw the social worker's small car.

Through the open kitchen door he saw the young woman walking up the path from the lane. She glanced at the bulging plastic bags, then at the boy's face.

'You're ready packed,' she remarked.

He was silent, not knowing how to tell her that he was not going with her.

'I've come earlier than I said. I thought you should see your new home before it gets dark,' the young woman said. But the boy thought that she knew he had not meant to keep his promise, and that she had come early to prevent him from escaping.

'Have you got everything you want to take? There's room in the car for another two bags if there's anything else,' she said.

What the boy wanted to take with him was the bird. He said, 'Where'm I going?' Thinking he could run away from there just as well as from here.

'I can't find foster-parents just now. I'm taking you to the Children's Home. I expect you know some of the children there already. There are several in the school you go to.'

The boy did not answer this.

'It's only till your Gran gets better and can come back here to be with you,' she said.

'How long's that going to be?' he asked.

'I'm not sure. A week or two, perhaps a little more. You can ask for yourself. The hospital's not far from the Home. You'll be able to go and see your Gran. You could go today. Visiting's between six and eight.'

The boy said, 'Yes.'

'Shall we go, then? Can we lock everything up? Have you got the doorkey?'

The key hung on a string on a hook behind the door. The boy wanted still to say that he would not go, but it was difficult. The young woman was so sure that he was going with her. But his bird . . .!

She saw him hanging back.

'Ready? Haven't forgotten anything?'

He hadn't forgotten the cygnet. He was desperate. He said, 'Could I keep something at the Home?'

'What sort of thing? Of course, you'll have your own clothes. Books.'

'Could I keep . . . a pet?' He hated saying the word. The cygnet was not a pet, it was his wild creature, which he had looked after for three-quarters of a year.

The social worker sounded doubtful. 'Some of the children have rabbits. Guinea-pigs. Things like that. I'm not sure. You'll have to ask when you get there. Have you got a pet here? A dog? A cat?'

He said, 'No, But there's a bird.'

'A budgie? Wouldn't your neighbour look after it just for a time?'

'It's a swan. Out on a pool.' He was giving away his secret. He hadn't wanted to tell her.

'A swan? But if it's on a pool, it'll be all right, won't it? Swans can look after themselves.'

'You sure they can?'

'Of course. Haven't you seen them on the river? It'll be all right,' she repeated and opened the car door.

He got in, feeling like a traitor. Did she really know about swans? He did not know what else to do. He had to go with her. But he would come back as soon as he could.

He thought about his cygnet all that day, during the drive to the Children's Home and for the rest of the afternoon and evening, while he was being greeted by the House Mother and Father and introduced to the other children. He hardly looked at the bed he was to sleep in, or the locker where he was to keep his clothes. He sat in the big bare room called the playroom with the other children while they watched the television screen; but although he had hardly seen any television programmes except at school, he did not attend. He was wondering what would happen to the cygnet, which had never spent a night out in the open before. Where would it sleep? Would it die of cold? Would some enemy attack it in the darkness? He was uneasy. He was miserable.

Before the programme was finished, the social worker had come back to take him to the hospital to see the old woman. They were told to go up in a lift that smelled of disinfectant, and from there they were let into a long ward, full of beds. The boy saw green walls, high, narrow windows, uncurtained, showing black sky outside. Some women were sitting in chairs, wearing dressing-gowns, others were occupying the beds. The ward was humming with visitors, carrying flowers, bunches of grapes, boxes of sweets. There was no one by the old woman's bed, and she was not sitting up. She lay still, under humped bedclothes, her eyes shut.

The young woman touched her on the shoulder, but she did not move. The young woman shook her gently, and she opened her eyes.

'Mrs Aishe? I've brought your grandson to see you,' the young woman said.

'She's deaf. She doesn't hear,' the boy said. But the old woman's eyes had turned towards him. She did not smile. She did not speak. She shut her eyes again. It was if she had said, 'I don't want to see you.'

'Perhaps we'd better wait a little. Your Gran seems very tired,' the young woman said.

The boy knew that the old woman would not want to see him however long they waited, but he did not say so. He and the young woman stood by the bed for another twenty minutes. The old woman snored. Presently a nurse came by.

'Not having much luck?' she asked. Her voice was bright. 'She doesn't care about any of us,' the boy thought.

54

'Has Mrs Aishe been awake during the day?' the social worker asked.

'I don't know. I've only just come on duty. I daresay she's still a bit woozy from the operation. It was only yesterday,' the nurse said, and she went off down the ward.

'I'm sorry. I'll take you back. We could try again tomorrow,' the young woman said, and she and the boy left the long ward and the buzz of conversation and she drove him back to the Children's Home.

'You'll be all right here?' she asked when he got out of the car.

'I want to go back home,' the boy said.

'As soon as your Gran is well enough,' she said, and left him.

The next morning, the boy started from the Home with the other children, to go to school. But before they reached the school gates, he had slipped away from the crocodile trail and hidden in a doorway. When the others were out of sight, he turned towards the familiar road, and by mid-morning he was on the further side of the duckpond and the post-office, on his way to the pool.

It was almost a year since he had come here first, and that day had been like this one, grey, stormy, cold. He saw the water reflecting the colourless, tinny light from the overcast sky. He saw nothing else. The pool was empty. Only the chilly wind raised a fretful trembling of its surface, even the moorhens were not there. His heart sank, he felt a black despair. His cygnet had gone. He would never see it again. If he were to search around, he might find its dead, marauded body lying somewhere on the mud among the reeds.

He could not bear to look.

He was watching, in a daze of misery, when he saw a movement among the reeds on the further side of the pool. He held his breath, and saw, not his pale brown cygnet, but a full-grown swan, silver-white, swim out into the open water. For a moment, he almost believed that it was magic, that overnight his young bird had reached maturity. But then, immediately behind the first bird, he saw another, and recognised the female following her mate. A new swan pair had discovered his secret pool. Perhaps they meant to nest here, to bring up a new family.

Now his fears for the cygnet grew again. He thought that the adult male might have attacked the cygnet, wanting the territory for itself. If the young bird had been driven away, could it have flown far? Where might it have gone?

He had no idea what an adult male swan might do to a young bird which didn't belong to him. He was bewildered. Then he thought of the cygnet's response to his call, and he whistled. He whistled the rising notes which the young bird had come to recognise.

He had not dared to hope. But the magic was at work again. From another side of the pool a smaller, darker bird came quickly across the water. The boy knelt on the muddy shore and held out his arms, and his cygnet came directly to him and laid its head on his shoulder.

The boy sobbed with relief and with love. The cygnet caressed his neck and his face with gentle tweaks of its beak.

The swan pair took no notice of the boy and his bird. They swam about the pool, dipping their necks into the deeper water in the middle, feeding.

After a time, the boy stood up. He was rigid with cold, sick with relief. The cygnet would be as safe here as on the duck-pond; safer, because it was not near traffic or human predators. He thought that perhaps the adult pair had adopted it and would look after it. He watched it take again to the water, then he turned back to the road.

When he got back to the Home, he found it deserted by everyone except one of the junior matrons. He was in disgrace, he found, for disappearing. 'His' social worker came in that evening to talk to him. She did not seem angry, or even surprised. Perhaps she had guessed that he would try to get away. She told him that if he made a habit of running away, she would have to find another place for him, further away and where he would be more strictly supervised.

'How long do I have to stay here?' the boy asked.

'I don't know yet. Do you want to go and visit your Gran tonight?'

'No.'

'Tomorrow?'

'She doesn't want to see me,' the boy said.

'It's difficult for her being deaf. As well as old. And ill.'

'All right. Tomorrow,' the boy said.

'You won't run away again before I come to fetch you?'

'No,' the boy said, and this time he meant it.

It was a relief to him that he had to go to school the next day. He was used to the school, he could bear to be there. But he did not like the Children's Home. It was not a bad place. The House Parents were kind, the children were like all other children, a mixed lot. But he felt that it was a prison. There were rules he could not remember. He was in a town, instead of being out in the country. He did not like the food, though it was good and there was plenty of it. But he could not get used to the never being alone. Whatever he did, wherever he was, there were always other people round him; talking, whistling, shouting, whispering. Even at night he could feel that there were sleeping bodies in the same room. He felt crowded, harassed. When 'his' social worker came to see him and asked if he were settling in, all he could say was, 'How long do I have to stay here?' A question she could not answer.

She took him again to the hospital, but the old woman still lay with her eyes shut and would not look at him. The boy thought, 'She could be there for weeks yet. And I have to stay in the Home till she is better.'

At the weekend, he asked for permission to go for a walk. He went back to the secret pool. The swan pair were there, their white feathers ruffled against the biting wind. His cygnet was there. He stayed as long as he could, watching it. It was a big bird now, grey-brown, but beginning to show the long neck and the easy swimming gait of the adult birds. He did not like to leave it at the end of the afternoon, but his mind was easier now about its safety. When the old woman was well again and they were back in the cottage, he would be able to visit it every day.

VIII

Weeks went by. The boy did not like the Children's Home any better, but he was not in a rage against it all the time. When he was not in school, he felt a dull ache of misery which he could try to forget. Two things made life a little easier: one was that on some weekends he was allowed to go by himself for a walk. Then he always visited the secret pool and saw the cygnet, safe and growing fast. The other was that there were books in the Home. The boy had never been able to get at so many books. He spent most of his time reading. He watched the television sometimes with the other children, but they often annoyed him by talking through the programmes. He was used to more silence than these children had ever heard. He liked best to be left alone to read.

When the social worker took him to the hospital, he could see that the old woman was not getting better. During one visit he noticed that her mouth was slewed strangely sideways and she snored loudly.

'What is it?' the boy asked, not liking to look at her.

'She's had a stroke,' the young woman said.

'Is that bad?'

'Lots of people have strokes and they get quite well again,' the young woman said. But the boy did not think the old woman would ever be well again.

When the young woman took him back to the Children's Home that evening, she said, 'I have to say goodbye.'

'Won't you be coming next week?' the boy asked.

'I'm leaving my job here and going back to London. I'm going to get married and work there,' she said.

The boy wanted to say he was sorry, but he did not know how.

'Mr Tomlinson will be looking after you instead of me. I hope you'll get on well together,' she said.

The boy noticed that she did not say, as most people would have, 'You *will* get on, you *will* like each other,' as if saying would make it so.

'He's coming to see you tomorrow,' she said. Then she held out her hand. 'Goodbye. I liked knowing you. Good luck.'

He shook her hand. He still could not say what he wanted to.

Before she shut the car door and drove off, she leant again out of the driving-seat. 'I forgot to ask before. How is your swan getting on?'

'She's all right,' the boy said. Then the young woman went. He was glad she had remembered the swan. But he wished she hadn't gone. Although he hadn't seen her more than twice a week, he felt lonely without her.

When he was back in the Home, he realised that he had called his cygnet 'she'. Without noticing it, he had known that she was not going to become the cob, the male bird. She would be a pen, a female, in time a mother swan.

He did not dislike Mr Tomlinson, but he did not like him as much as he had liked the young woman. He did not find it easy to talk to him. The next week, Mr Tomlinson came to the Home and the boy was called to see him in a room by themselves.

'I'm afraid I have bad news,' Mr Tomlinson said.

The boy waited.

'Your grandmother isn't going to get better.'

The boy agreed. 'No.'

'In fact . . . she is dying.'

The boy waited again.

'Well . . . She died this morning. It was quite peaceful.'

'Yes,' the boy said.

He felt the man look at him to see if he was going to cry. But he was not. He felt nothing about the old woman. All he wanted was to know what would happen next.

'Do I have to stay here?' he asked.

'Just for now, you do. Until we find out whether there is any family you might belong to.'

'There isn't anyone,' the boy said.

'I'm going to have a look in your old cottage. Your Gran may have kept papers there that might tell us something.'

The boy thought of the photograph he had taken. He said, 'Can I come and look too?'

'That's a good idea! You can show me where she kept everything. I'll take you out next Saturday, when you're not in school.'

When they were driving along the straight road between the sedge and the dunes, the young man asked, 'Did your Gran ever tell you anything? About your people? Or hers?'

'No.'

'Didn't she ever talk about when she was young? Or about your Mum or your Dad?'

The boy said, 'No,' again.

He thought, 'While he's looking through the papers, I'll go and look at the pool.'

In the cottage, the boy showed Mr Tomlinson the drawers in the upstairs room where he had seen the envelopes of papers. He helped to carry them down to the kitchen. Mr Tomlinson sat at the table, and spread the papers out in front of him, reading them carefully. For a time, the boy sat opposite to him, watching. Then he said, 'I'm going for a walk.'

'Don't be too long. I'd like to start back in another half hour,' the young man said.

The boy went out to the sedgy marshlands and took the track that led to the secret pool. He had been there two weeks before, and this time the only difference was that Spring had come to the marshes. He saw pussy-willows in the hedge by the road, the air was soft on his face, and there were small spindly white flowers in the grass. On the pool the adult swans floated with the same dignity and grace that he had first noticed in the pair he had seen on the estuary, whose one child he had rescued. He saw his cygnet too, busy dabbling for food. She came to him when he whistled. He stroked her soft plumage and he loved her. He whispered, 'I'll fetch you soon. I'll find somewhere we can be together.' But he did not know how he could keep this promise, and he left the pool sad that he could not take her with him at once.

When he got back to the cottage, the young man was tying up bundles of papers, ready to stack in his car.

He held out a photograph to the boy. 'Ever seen this? D'you know who these people are?'

The boy saw the picture of a woman sitting on a country

stile. A man stood beside her, and on her lap she held a little girl with straight dark hair.

'I don't know,' he said.

'Could that be your Gran?'

The boy looked more closely. But he had known the old woman only when her hair had been grey and her face set in harsh lines of age and bitterness.

He said, 'I suppose it could be. A long time ago.' He looked at the back of the photograph, but there was nothing written there.

'I'll take all this stuff back with me and go through it carefully. I expect we'll be able to find something that'll help,' Mr Tomlinson said.

'Suppose you don't find anything?' the boy said.

'We'll see you're taken care of. Don't worry,' the young man said.

He took the boy back to the Children's Home. The boy wondered how much longer he could bear to stay there. The young man saw his face and said again, 'Don't worry. There's probably someone belonging to you.'

The boy thought about belonging. Had he belonged to the old woman? Had she belonged to him? He did not feel as if either had belonged to the other. The only thing that had ever belonged to him was the cygnet, and even that not so much now that they could not see each other every day.

IX

The boy had not hoped much from Mr Tomlinson's search for anyone 'belonging' to him, and as weeks, and then months, went by, he began to believe that he must stay in the Home for ever. Until he was old enough to leave school and try to find a job. He did not get used to the Home, the crowd, the noise. He did not say how much he hated it. He behaved like the other boys, except that he did not talk much and shouted only when he was angry. He fought for his rights if he had to, he was not bullied or teased. But he did not make friends. He felt locked up inside, just as his body was locked up in the Home. He knew that the cottage had been sold and he could not go back there. He managed sometimes to visit the secret pool, and each time the sight of his bird made him feel a little better. But he was lonely, among all the other children, in a way he had never felt lonely in the cottage. The House Mother and Father tried to be kind to him, but they found him sullen. He did not respond to their questions or their sympathy. 'Don't you have any feelings — Don't you miss your Gran?' the House Father asked him one day, and when the boy told the truth and said, 'No,' he saw that the man was shocked.

The summer came. On the secret pool the grown pair of

swans had raised a family of five babies. The boy looked at them swimming behind their parents, sheltering under their wings, riding on their backs. He ached for his cygnet who, like him, had no parents. But the half-grown cygnet did not seem to care. She would still come when the boy whistled, and would caress him, and then the boy felt comforted for a little while.

The summer holidays began. The boy went to camp with eleven other boys. He quite liked living out of doors and learning about wild birds and animals, and how to light fires and cook and to look after himself away from houses and the way people lived in them. He imagined himself living always like this, near water, where he would look after birds and mend their broken wings, take fish-hooks out of their necks, as he had seen on the video on television about swans. When he went back to the village and the Children's Home he was bored, and several times he left without permission, to go for long solitary walks, sometimes to the pool, sometimes to the estuary to watch a colony of swans there and to watch the fishermen, hating them for the lead weights they had used, which, he now knew, had probably been the reason why 'his' swan pair had died.

One wet day, when he was looking through his locker for a penknife he had lost, he found the photograph he had taken from the old woman's possessions in the cottage, after her accident. He looked again at the face of the girl, Jennie, and wondered who she was. He wondered if she could have been the old woman herself when she was quite young. Could she ever have smiled like that? Had she ever looked as if she loved life, as this girl did? He turned the picture over to see the name, 'Jennie' again, and found that he was holding another piece of paper on the back. It must have been in the envelope with the picture and he had not noticed that besides the photograph, he had brought away with him the marriage form which had told him that Violet Aishe had married Walter Bridwell.

It did not seem important. Violet Aishe must have been some sort of relation, and he did not know why the old woman should have kept this form, when she seemed to have kept nothing among her papers that could help the social worker to trace her family. He put the form back with the photograph and hid them among his other things, then forgot them as he had forgotten them before.

He was reminded of them a month or two later. It was autumn, school had begun again. Mr Tomlinson had come to see him, apologising yet again for his failure to have any news. 'I thought by now we'd have been able to find out something. There was a family by your name, lived not so very far away a long time ago. But they moved and no one seems to know what became of them.'

The boy remembered. He said, 'There was someone called Violet Aishe.'

'That's right. That was your grandmother.'

Violet? That old, deaf woman, had been called Violet? He said, 'No. This one married someone.'

'How do you know that?' Mr Tomlinson asked.

'There's a paper. I'd forgotten I had it.'

'Have you still got it?'

'It's in my locker. Upstairs.'

'Fetch it down, will you? That might be just what we want,' Mr Tomlinson said. When the boy showed it to him — but he would not show the photograph of Jennie — the young

68

man studied the yellowed form. 'St John's Church, Hackney. That's where she got married, then. Nineteen-thirty. That'd be about right. That must've been your Gran. Where did you say you found this?'

'It was in the chest of drawers upstairs. I didn't mean to take it away. It got muddled up with some other things I had.'

'Don't count too much on it . . . but it just might be what we need. I'll take it with me, if you don't mind.'

The boy didn't mind. He couldn't believe the marriage form had anything to do with him.

Later, not long before Christmas, which would be the first Christmas the boy would spend in the Home, the social worker called to see him, and the boy saw at once that something had happened. The young man was different. He looked excited. He said, 'I've got news for you.'

'What?'

'I was right. That was your Gran's marriage certificate. She married Walter Bridwell and she went to live in Hackney, where he came from.'

'She was called Aishe,' the boy said.

'Before she married, she was. Then, when she came back here to live, she went back to her maiden name. The one she was born with.'

'Why?' the boy asked.

'She hadn't stayed married long. Her husband left her. But she'd had a baby. A daughter. Jennifer.'

The boy remembered the picture of the smiling girl.

'She's your Mum.'

The boy trembled. He did not speak.

'Jennifer Bridwell. She was born in Hackney, we've found the registration of her birth. Now we're looking for her.'

The boy wanted to ask why it had been his Gran that brought him up. If he had a Mum, what had she been doing? But he could not make himself ask.

The young man stood up. 'I'll be back. I might have some good news for you some time. But don't count on it, being before Christmas. These things can take time, and everyone's busy just now.'

Everyone was busy because it was nearly Christmas time. The boy knew that. People with proper families, not pretend parents like the House Mother and Father, kind as they tried to be, were getting ready for Christmas. Wrapping presents, sending cards, arranging parties where there would be fathers and mothers and uncles and aunts, brothers and sisters. Grandparents and babies.

He did not want to think about all that.

He endured the Christmas in the Home, where half the children were away with friends or relatives; for those who were left, there were, it was true, presents and parties, a visit to the pantomime and another to the circus. It was not all miserable, but there was a feeling in him, underneath any excitement or enjoyment he might have, that this was only a pretence at the real thing. The real thing, which was belonging, and knowing that you belonged, was going on somewhere else.

The Christmas holidays passed. School began again. He had been in the Home for nearly a year. He was still not used to it, not reconciled. Mr Tomlinson did not reappear.

X

At last he went to see the House Father.

'Could I have an animal here? To keep?' he asked.

The House Father was pleased. 'A pet! Of course. Why not, if it makes you feel more at home with us? What would you like? A rabbit? We might be able to manage a white rat.'

The boy despised rabbits and he did not want a rat. He said, 'I want to have a swan.'

The House Father was taken aback. 'You couldn't get a swan.'

'I know of one. It's tame.'

'A tame swan! Where is it?'

'Near where I used to live.'

'Swans aren't tame,' the man said.

'This one is. It would come if I called it.'

'We've never had a swan. You mean it's really . . . domesticated? Tame?' the House Father asked again.

'I'm sure.'

'Of course we do have the river.' He meant the small stream that ran at the end of the garden of the Children's Home, where they fished for minnows and splashed about in hot weather. 'Would it be safe? We couldn't have a bird that might attack the little ones.'

'It wouldn't hurt anyone if it was left alone,' the boy said.

'How would you get it here?'

'I could fetch it. It knows me,' the boy said.

The House Father asked more questions. Did the swan belong to anyone? How had it become tame? He saw that the boy was eager as he had not been eager about anything since he had come to the Home a year ago, and in the end he agreed. 'I must find out from the RSPCA whether it will be all right to move a swan,' he said.

The boy did not know what the RSPCA was, but he was pleased with the permission to have his cygnet near him. Later in the day he went through the grounds to the stream and stayed there till early dark, imagining his bird on this water. It wasn't very deep, even a small bird could reach the bottom easily; the branches of the trees met overhead, and in summer when the leaves were out it would be shaded like the inside of a great arched church. More secret even than the pool. The roots of the trees were exposed by the water's eating away of the overhanging banks, and there were holes between the twisted roots which would make good hiding places.

'The swan will be happy here. I shall see her every day,' the boy said out loud, as if he needed to convince himself.

The more the House Father thought about the idea of having a pet as unusual as a swan, the better he liked it. He told some of the other children that they might soon have a swan living in the stream. The boy found that suddenly he was popular. Boys and girls came to him wanting to know how he had found the swan. How had he caught it? How had he tamed it? Where was it now? When would he bring it to the Home? What was its name? Was it dangerous? Was it true that a blow from a swan's wing could break a man's arm?

The boy did not answer the questions. He said, 'Wait till you see it.' Their questions made him uneasy, but he was also excited and proud. He had never been a hero before.

Since he could not carry the swan for the two miles from the pool to the Home, he had to wait until there was a weekend when the House Father had time to drive him in the van which belonged to the Home. So it was the end of February, and a soft, Spring day, when they drove through the town and out along the road that led to the cottage where the boy had lived with old woman.

'Is this it? Is this where you used to live?' the House Father asked when they came to the post-office and the duckpond. But the boy said, 'No. Go a bit further. I'll tell you when to stop.'

He waited until they were very near the group of cottages, then said, 'Here! You wait, I'll be back in a minute.' He did not want anyone to see him take the track to the secret pool. He set off back down the road by which they had just come, then turned off on the path to the pool.

Because he had been waiting for this expedition to carry the swan back with him, he had not been to the pool for over a month. When he got there, he saw his swan first. She was in the middle of the pool, her neck long enough now for her to feed in the deeper water, her plumage moon-white, shining on the grey water. She had not heard his approach. She was preening her wing feathers, her neck curved back like a huge S, her eyes half shut.

Beyond her, he saw the swan pair, and scattered over the rest of the water there were the half-grown cygnets, dun brown, busily feeding. When he looked at them, he wondered that he had thought his cygnet beautiful when she had been

like these scurrying youngsters. Compared to her full-grown majesty, they were nothing. Ordinary, dull little birds. He gazed on his swan and his heart swelled with pride.

Then he saw another swan on the pool.

A full-grown cob, a male, had come out of the reeds and

was approaching his swan. She turned her head and went towards him. The boy saw them greet each other, bow their heads. They laid their necks together. The cob preened the feathers of the pen's neck, she smoothed his head with her bill. There was no doubt, the boy knew, that he was watching the courtship of this young pair.

Rage burned in his heart.

This was his swan. He had rescued her, before she was hatched, from certain death. He had watched over her, guarded her as well as he could, thought about her, longed for her. She belonged to him. He did not want to lose her now that she was grown and beautiful.

He whistled.

She turned her head and swam quickly towards him. As before, she came up the sloping mud-flat to him into his arms. He felt the warmth, the weight of her body. He ran his hand down her silky neck, he stroked her wings. He laid his cheek on top of her head. It was satin-smooth.

The young male was disturbed. He had swum close to the water's edge. He stretched his neck and hissed at the boy. He felt the female move restlessly. He tightened the hold of his arms around her, but she continued to turn her head to look away from him, at the young male on the pool. Then she turned back and her beak just nibbled his left ear.

Four yards away, the male hissed again. He came half out of the water, and spread his wings. It was meant to be a frightening sight, and the boy was frightened. But he noticed that the bird did not come closer. He must have realised that the pen was not in danger, and he could not attack the boy without also attacking her.

The boy released his swan and walked a little way from the

pool. Both swans watched him. He whistled softly, and the female took a step or two towards him. He walked a little further, and whistled again. Again she followed a short way. The boy thought, 'I could get her away from the pool, near to the road. Then I could pick her up and carry her to the van. Once we were in the van we'd be safe.'

She was his swan.

For nearly two years he had planned his free time around her. He had taken risks for her, broken promises for her, loved her as he had never loved anyone or anything. All this made her belong to him. She was his swan.

He thought of her in the stream at the end of the grounds of the Children's Home. He would be able to see her every day. She would be safer there than out here on the sedge. The other children would like to have her there. He would tell them not to frighten her, to leave her alone. They would see that she would come at his whistle, that she knew and trusted him.

She was his swan.

'The prince stole the mantle of feathers that belonged to the swan princess. Then she could not change herself back into a swan, but had to remain a beautiful girl, unable to fly away. The prince married her and they lived happily ever after.'

Nonsense! A fairy story.

They mate for life.

But his bird's mother swan had not died of a broken heart as he had once imagined. She had died of lead poisoning, and so had the male, her mate. Probably that story of their fidelity to each other was just as much made up, silly, soppy stuff, as the tale about the swan princess or about swans singing before they died. He knew from his own observation that that was not true.

He remembered the anglers who sat on the bank, upstream from the Children's Home. He did not think that any lead they might use for their weights would be carried by the water as far as the grounds of the Home.

He stood for what seemed a long time among the reeds. He saw his swan turn back to the pool. He did not whistle for her again.

The van was waiting when he got back to the road. The House Father was standing by it, with the Sunday paper

spread out on its bonnet. It was a very still afternoon. There was no wind to ruffle the leaves of the newspaper.

'Hi! You've been long enough. Where's your swan?' he said, when he saw the boy.

'She wasn't there,' the boy said.

'Gone off? You were waiting for it, were you?'

'I waited for a bit.'

'Want to try again? I don't mind staying here for another twenty minutes, half an hour. It'd be fine to have a swan at the Home. The kids would love it.'

'It's no good waiting,' the boy said, and climbed into the van.

'Gone back to the estuary, probably. There's a whole lot of swans there. Never mind. We could come back another time, if you like,' the man said. He started the engine, let in the clutch, and the van began to roll down the road.

The boy did not answer. He kept his face turned towards the window, away from the man. He was cold, in spite of the Spring-like weather, but the tears running down his face were bitter and hot.

XI

The boy was miserable. He was angry with himself and with everything. He became aggressive. He hit two other boys and sulked. He hardly ate. The House Father, believing this was the effect of his disppointment about the swan, offered to drive him back to the road near the cottage in another two weeks' time. When the boy refused, the man suggested that he might like to have a guinea-pig of his very own. The boy sulked still more.

And then the magic thing happened.

The boy was sent for to the House Parents' private room. The young man, the social worker was there, and the boy saw that he was excited. So was the House Mother.

'Here he is,' she said.

'Hi!' the young man said. The boy did not answer.

'He's got news for you,' the House Mother said.

'I've got news,' the young man said.

The boy looked from one to the other. He thought of his swan. Had they found her? Had she followed him? Followed the van, could not bear to let him go? He did not speak. He waited.

'We've found someone,' the young man said.

The boy knew what was coming.

'We've found your Gran's family.'

The boy's disappointment rose in him like sickness. His tongue tasted horrible, his throat burned.

'We have found her daughter.'

Silence. The House Mother fidgeted in her chair.

'We've found your mother. Your Mum.'

'My Mum?' the boy said.

'It took a long time. We had to make quite sure we'd got the right person. Your Mum.'

The boy could not understand what they were saying. There were words which seemed to mean nothing to him. He heard, 'Salvation Army', 'solicitors', 'advertisement', 'Married now, two kids', and other sentences which buzzed in his ears, while he thought, 'My Mum? I've never had a Mum.'

'Wants to take you home,' the young man was saying.

'A Home?' The boy had had enough of Homes.

'Not a Home like this. Her home, your Mum's house, where she lives with her family,' the House Mother said.

'Her family?'

'You'll have a Mum and a Dad of your very own.'

The boy still could not understand.

'She's coming here to see you. This afternoon.'

He was dazed. How could a Mum suddenly appear now, out of nowhere? He left the House Mother's room, and the social worker came after him.

'Bit of a surprise, isn't it? I expect you'll want time to think about it.'

The boy nodded.

'I just wanted to say. See how you and she get on. You don't have to go with her at once. She wants to have you all right, but . . . If you don't want that, you could probably stay on here. For a bit, anyway. She's agreed to that. After all, you don't know each other, do you?'

'No,'

'Well! See how it goes.'

At last the boy asked, 'Why . . .? Why . . .?'

'Why did she let you go when you were a baby?'

'Why?'

'She was only a kid herself. Didn't know what to do. She and your Gran — that was her mother, see? — they'd never got on. Your Gran told her she'd have to let you go for adoption and she'd see to it. She took you off with her, and your Mum thought she'd taken you somewhere to get you adopted. Didn't know where and didn't ask. Girls do feel like that sometimes. Can't bear to know. Anyway, she's dead keen to meet you now. But as I was saying, you don't have to decide anything right away.'

The boy did not know how to meet the unknown woman who was his Mum. He asked no more questions. He waited.

That autumn he was at school in London.

'That's not really your Mum,' one of his new schoolmates said.

'Yes, she is,' the boy said.

'She doesn't look old enough. I thought she was your sister.'

'My sisters are little kids. She's my Mum all right.' He was positive.

'You call her Jennie.'

'That's her name.'

'Seems funny you don't call her Mum.'

'She likes me calling her Jennie.'

The boy liked it. But his father, he called Dad, and that was right too.

'So that's where you and she lived,' Jennie said, outside the cottage, which now belonged to other people.

'It didn't look that way then,' the boy said. The windows were polished, and the paintwork was new. The garden was tidy and planted out, and a neat fence divided it from Mrs Dix's next door.

'It's more'n a year since you left. No, two. I was forgetting the Home.' It was summer again.

'Were you happy here with her?' the woman asked.

'She wasn't bad to me,' the boy said. He asked, 'Was she bad to you, when you were a kid?' He was learning now to ask questions.

'She didn't mean to be. After my Dad had left her . . . it wasn't so good. I'd always got on better with him than with her.'

'You let her take me,' the boy said.

'For the adoption people. Everyone said it'd be the best for you. I never dreamed she'd keep you.'

'Did you miss me?' he asked.

'Sort of. At the start. But I knew I couldn't keep you. I was at school still, see? There didn't seem anything else to do. But later . . .'

'Later?' the boy prompted.

'When we'd got married, your Dad and me. Then I wished I hadn't let you go. I didn't know I'd find you again, and it'd be all right.'

'It's all right,' the boy said.

They turned away from the tidy cottage. The woman said, 'Was it just the house you wanted to show me? Let's go and find Dad and the kids on the beach.'

The boy said, 'No, wait. There's something else.'

'I don't want to leave them too long.'

'It's not far. Just down the road.'

They walked down the road. The boy saw that the track to the secret pool was overgrown with long grass. It had not been used.

'Hi! Where're you going? That's just marsh.'

'It's all right. It's not muddy,' the boy said. He led, and the woman followed. He saw that the reeds round the pool were higher than ever.

'I suppose you know what you're doing?' the woman said.

'We're almost there.' He turned to look at her. 'It's a secret. You won't tell?'

'I won't tell.'

'Promise?'

'Promise.' She smiled at him. He was so serious. It had only just become possible to tease him gently, but this was not the right moment for teasing.

The boy pushed on a little further. Then the reflection of the bright sky on the water of the pool was dazzling. He held back a swathe of reeds to let her through. They looked together.

'Oh! Oh, look! Aren't they lovely? Swans!'

Stephen Bowkett
Spellbinder £1.75

'I'm scared of it, Tony. You don't know how far it can go'
'It's OK. I'm controlling it'
Tony lay in his usual place on the bank. A green glass marble rested
in the air, an inch above the ground.

Tony's interest in magic meant he had a few tricks up his sleeve. But
it was all an optical illusion – speed of the hand deceiving the eye.
Until one day he made a coin totally disappear. Not even Tony knew
what was happening then, and it made him shiver.

   When the school fete needed a professional magician, Tony was
asked to ring one. As he dialled, his heart began to thump. Someone
picked up the phone, and before he could utter a word, the voice
said: 'Hello Tony. I've waited for your call.'

What was happening was real magic.

Betsy Byars
The Not-Just-Anybody Family £1.95

Boy breaks into city jail

It made all the headlines when Vern broke *into* prison, but what
would you do if your grandpa was in jail? The Blossoms had no
doubts. Since they couldn't get Pap out, Maggie and Vern had to
get in. A little unusual, perhaps, but as Maggie said, 'We Blossoms
have never been just "anybody".'

This is the first adventure for the Blossoms — Pap, Vern, Maggie,
Junior and Mud the dog. They're a family you won't forget.

Joyce Dunbar
Mundo and the Weather-Child £1.95

'I hate the garden! I hate the house! I want to go back home.'

Edmund feels a stranger in the rambling house he and his parents have moved to, but by the time winter arrives, he is utterly lost. Unable to hear, he is locked into a solitary world of silence.

But, slowly, he discovers another world in the wild garden. There he makes friends with the Weather-Child, who climbs and rides on the weather, swinging on all its changes.

It is the Weather-Child who frees him from isolation and leads him back into the real world.

Rose Tremain
Journey to the Volcano £1.95

'As they swam, their eyes stayed fixed on the volcano.' The black
cloud sat tight on its rim. Then, up through the black cloud and
spurting high into the clear sky above it came a gush of flame,
higher than any fountain, brighter than any firework . . .
'"She's going!" cried Guido.'

Trouble had been brewing all summer, from the day George's mother
left his father and snatched George from his London school.
Escaping to his mother's old home on the slopes of Mount Etna,
George found himself plunged into the heart of a large family he
barely knew. Life on the mountain was exciting and different. But
under the sunny slopes lay a seething mass of molten lava, waiting
to erupt . . .

All Pan books are available at your local bookshop or newsagent, or can be ordered direct from the publisher. Indicate the number of copies required and fill in the form below.

Send to: **CS Department, Pan Books Ltd., P.O. Box 40, Basingstoke, Hants. RG21 2YT.**

or phone: 0256 469551 (Ansaphone), quoting title, author and Credit Card number.

Please enclose a remittance* to the value of the cover price plus: 60p for the first book plus 30p per copy for each additional book ordered to a maximum charge of £2.40 to cover postage and packing.

*Payment may be made in sterling by UK personal cheque, postal order, sterling draft or international money order, made payable to Pan Books Ltd.

Alternatively by Barclaycard/Access:

Card No.   ⬚⬚⬚⬚⬚⬚⬚⬚⬚⬚⬚⬚⬚⬚⬚⬚⬚

Signature:

Applicable only in the UK and Republic of Ireland.

While every effort is made to keep prices low, it is sometimes necessary to increase prices at short notice. Pan Books reserve the right to show on covers and charge new retail prices which may differ from those advertised in the text or elsewhere.

NAME AND ADDRESS IN BLOCK LETTERS PLEASE:

....

Name —————————————————————————

Address —————————————————————————

————————————————————————————

————————————————————————————

————————————————————————————

3/87